 One of the most important ways children learn to read — and learn to *like* reading — is by being with readers. Every time you read aloud, read along, or listen to your child read, you are providing the support that she or he needs as an emerging reader.

Disney's First Readers were created to make that reading time fun for you and your child. Each book in this series features characters that most children already recognize from popular Disney films. The familiarity and appeal of these high-interest characters will draw emerging readers easily into the story and at the same time support basic literacy skills, such as understanding that print has meaning, connecting oral language to written language, and developing cueing systems. And because Disney's First Readers are highly visual, children have another tool to help in understanding the text. This makes early reading a comfortable, confident experience — exactly what emerging readers need to become successful, fluent readers.

Read to Your Child

Here are a few hints to make early reading enjoyable and educational:

★ Talk with children before reading. Let them see how much they already know about the Disney characters. If they are unfamiliar with the movie basis of a book, take a few minutes to look at the cover and some of the illustrations to establish a context. Talking is important, since oral language precedes and supports reading.

★ Run your finger along the text to show that the words carry the story. Let your child read along if she or he recognizes that there are repeated words or phrases.

★ Encourage questions. A child's questions are good clues to his or her comprehension or thinking strategies.

★ Be prepared to read the same book several times. Children will develop ease with the story and concepts, so that later they can concentrate on reading and language.

Let Your Child Read to You

You are your child's best audience, so encourage her or him to read aloud to you often. And:

★ If children ask about an unknown word, give it to them. Don't interrupt the flow of reading to have them sound it out. However, if children start to sound out a word, let them.

★ Praise all reading efforts warmly and often!

—Patricia Koppman
Past President
International Reading Association

For Jacqui, Howie, and Sharon
—J. K.

Printed in the United States of America.
First Edition
1 3 5 7 9 10 8 6 4 2
Library of Congress Catalog Card Number: 99-61190
ISBN: 0-7868-4358-6

Howdy, Sheriff Woody!

Written by
Judy Katschke

Illustrated by
the storybook artists
at Disney Publishing
Creative Development

Disney
PRESS

New York

One day Woody walked into a strange town.
"Hmm," Woody said.
"Looks like this town needs a sheriff!"

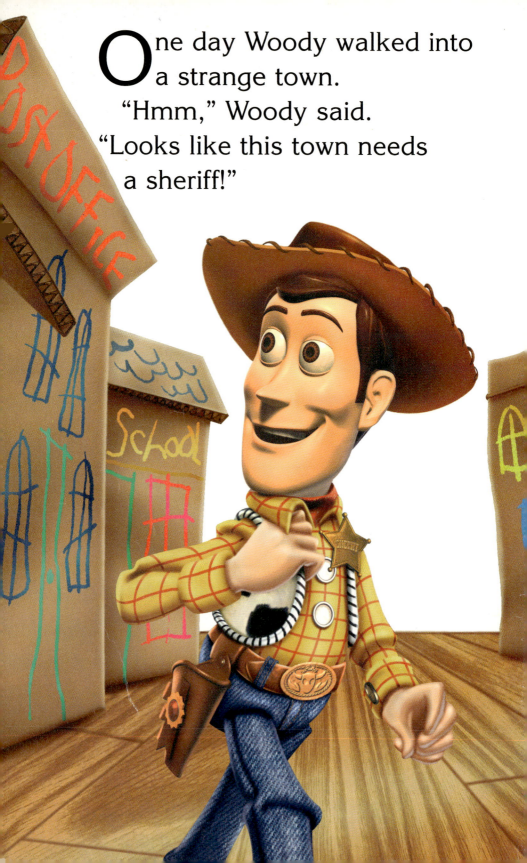

Woody hopped onto a bucket.
He yelled in his best cowboy voice:
"Howdy, strangers! I'm your new
sheriff, Woody!"

But there was nobody around.

Sheriff Woody checked out
the town. It *was* strange. . . .
"Hoo-eee!" Woody cried.
"That is the biggest armadillo
I ever saw!"

"That is no armadillo!" Woody said.
"It's a dinosaur!"
"Did I scare you?" Rex asked.

Woody saw a cowboy boot.
It shook like a possum with
the hiccups!
"Whoa!" Woody cried.
"There's a snake in that boot!"

But there was no snake in that boot!
It was just Green Army Men!

"Moving out of boot camp, Sheriff!" Sarge called.

"Move! Move! Move!"

Then Woody saw the strangest
thing of all. . . .

"Uh-oh!" Woody cried. "It looks like
a twister!"

"It's not a twister!" Jessie said. "It's me! And I am faster than a spinning top!"

"Let's see you top *that*!" she said to the sheriff.

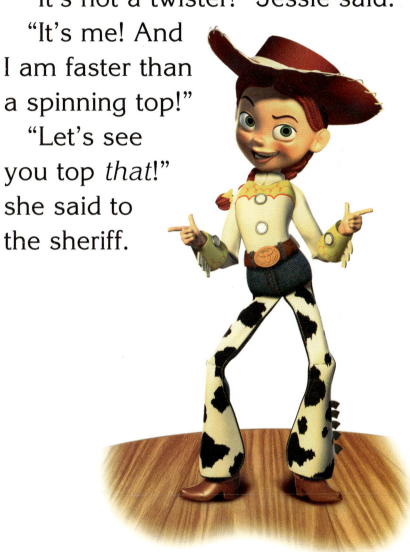

Woody liked this new town.
It had a store.
It had a school.
It even had a bank!
"That's me!" said Hamm.

Woody heard a sound.
Someone was
coming!

"Outlaws!" Hamm cried.
"Bandits!" Rex roared.
"Invaders!" The alien shivered.
"SPELL THE WORD *HELP*!!!"
Mr. Spell said.

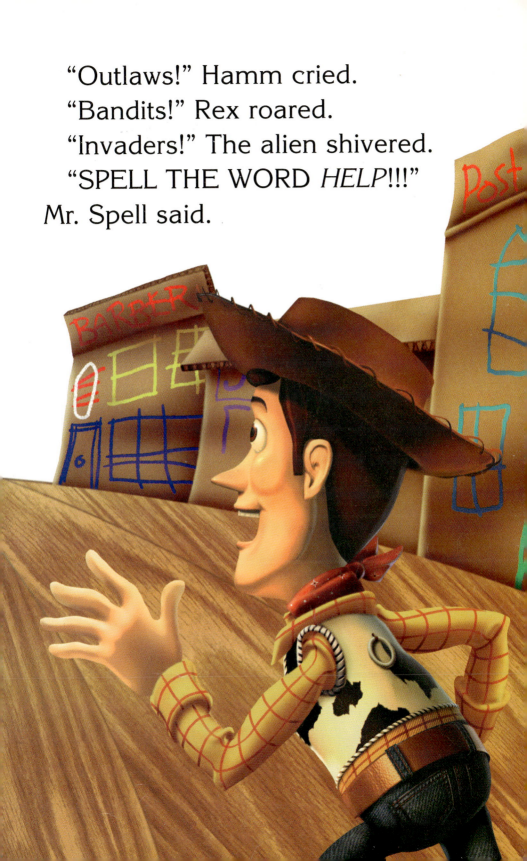

Woody looked at his badge.
It was his job to protect the town!

"Don't worry, folks!" Woody said.
"I'll show them what we're made of!"
"I think it's plastic," said Rex.

Woody was ready.
He stepped into the
dusty street.
"I wish I were that
brave!" Rex said.

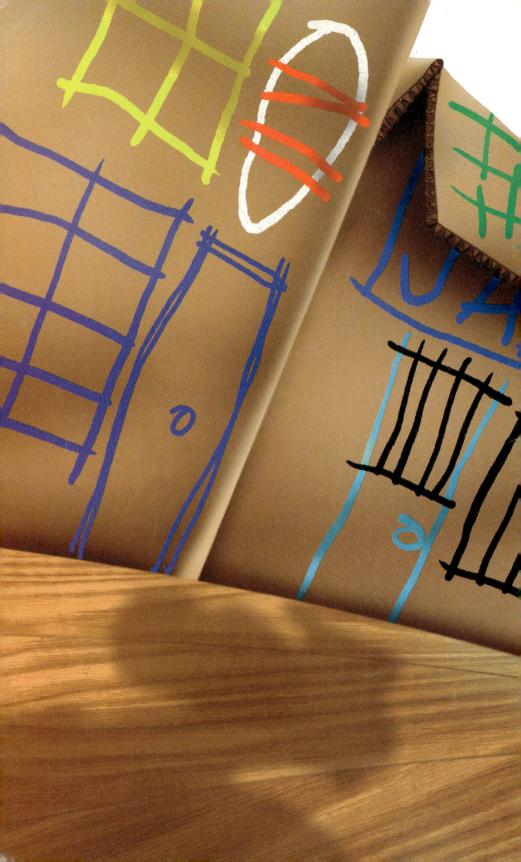

The sound got louder and louder.
Woody's heart beat faster and faster.

But just as Woody was about to draw,
the stranger rode into town. . . .

"Greetings! We come in peace!"
It was Buzz Lightyear and Bullseye!

Sheriff Woody smiled from
ear to ear.

"There are no strangers in
this town!" he said. "Only
friends!"